HOW TO WRITE A POEM

BY

KWAME ALEXANDER
AND
DEANNA NIKAIDO

Art by
MELISSA
SWEET

Quill Tree Books
An Imprint of HarperCollins Publishers

Quill
Tree Books is an imprint
of HarperCollins Publishers.
How to Write a Poem. Text copyright © 2023 by
KA Productions. Illustrations copyright © 2023 by Melissa
Sweet. All rights reserved. Manufactured in Italy. No part of
this book may be used or reproduced in any manner whatsoever
without written permission except in the case of brief quotations
embodied in critical articles and reviews. For information address
HarperCollins Children's Books, a division of HarperCollins Publishers,
195 Broadway, New York, NY 10007. www.harpercollinschildrens.com.
Library of Congress Control Number: 2022941739.
ISBN 978-0-06-306090-6. The artist used watercolor, gouache,
mixed media, handmade and vintage papers, and beach pebbles
to create the illustrations for this book. Hand lettered
by Melissa Sweet. Book design by Dana Fritts.
22 23 24 25 26 RTLO 10 9 8 7 6 5 4 3 2 1
First Edition

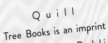

For
Kim Hardwick

—K.A. and D.N.

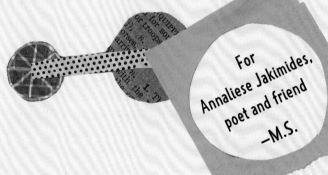

For
Annaliese Jakimides,
poet and friend

—M.S.

"WE ARE ALL
EITHER WHEELS OR
CONNECTORS.
WHICHEVER WE ARE,
WE MUST FIND
TRUTH AND BALANCE,
WHICH IS A
BICYCLE."
—NIKKI GIOVANNI

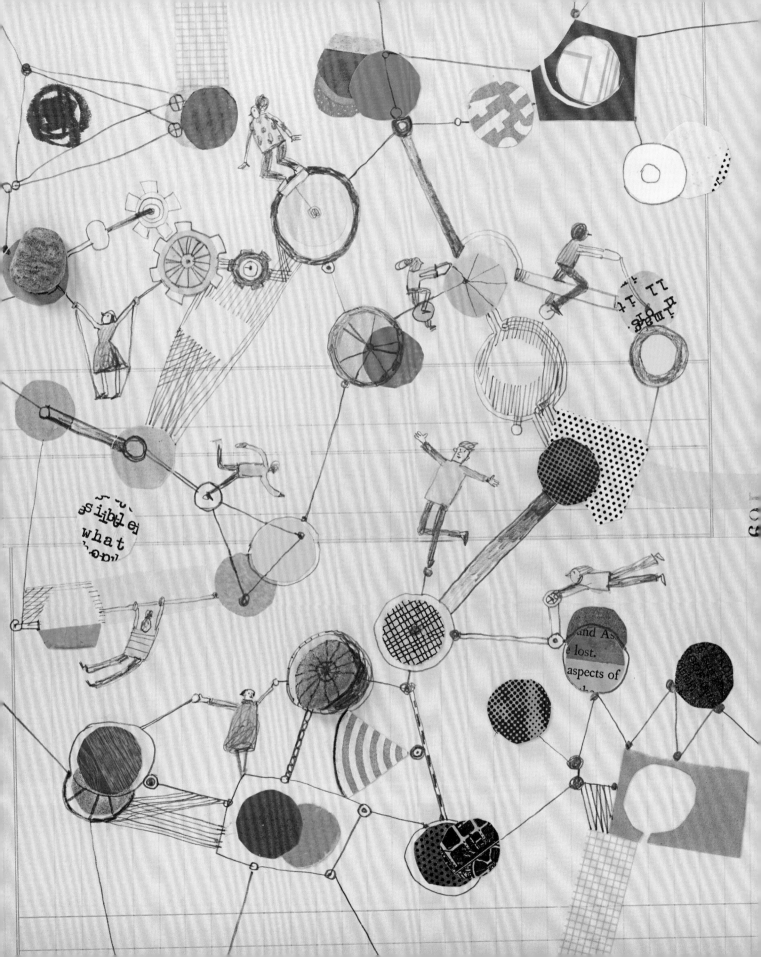

BEGiN

WiTH A QUESTION,

LIKE AN ACORN
WAITING FOR SPRING.

CLOSE YOUR EYES,

OPEN THE WINDOW

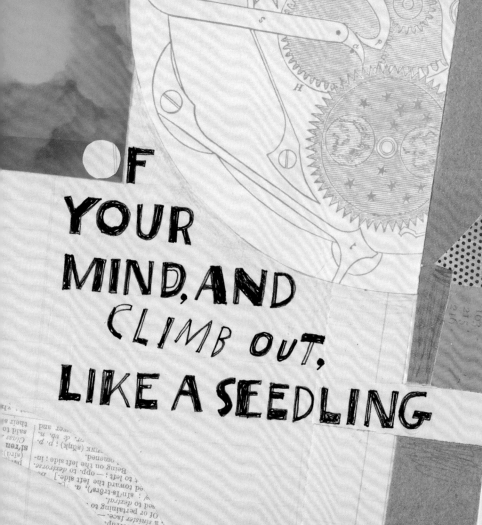

...OF YOUR MIND, AND CLIMB OUT, LIKE A SEEDLING

REACHING FOR TOMORROW.

NEXT, LISTEN TO THE GRASS, THE FLOWERS, THE TREES—ANYTHING

FEEL THEIR GLOW.
AND WHEN YOU THINK
YOU KNOW THE ANSWER,

light its young pure buds,
e bloom, (See: Lyric Poetry

LEAN INTO
THE ENDLESS SKY

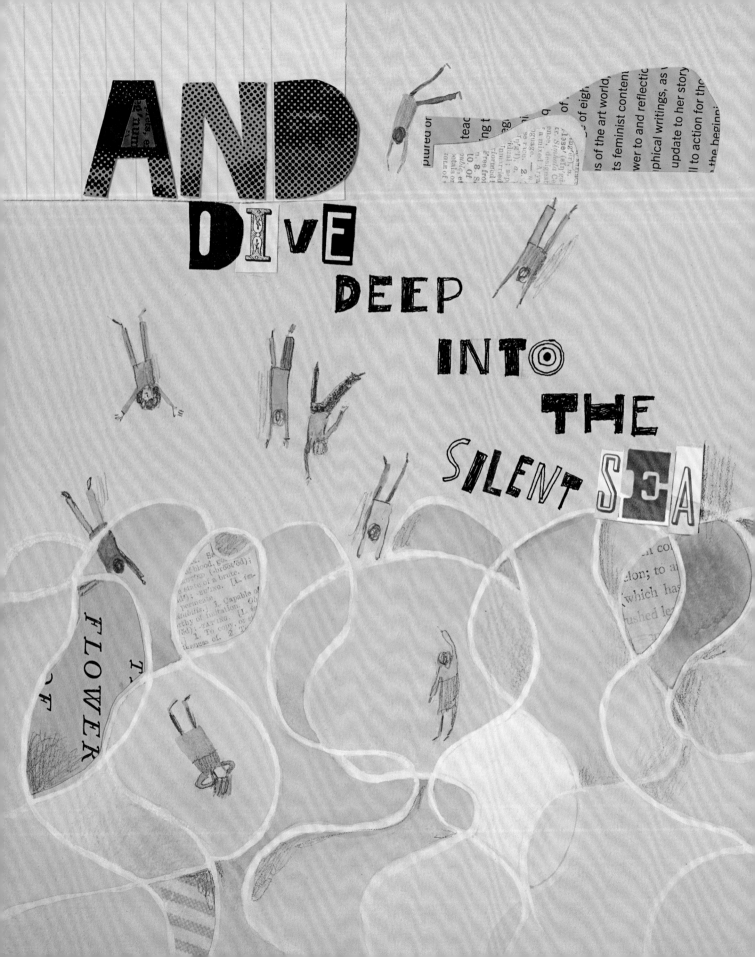

AND DIVE DEEP INTO THE SILENT SEA

TO DISCOVER A COTTON CANDY CAVALCADE OF SOUNDS—

INVITE THEM

INTO YOUR PAPER BOAT AND ROW ROW ROW

ACROSS THE WILD WHITE EXPANSE.

FOLLOW
THE BURNING STARS
AROUND THE CRYSTAL MOON.

LET THEM DANCE WITH YOUR JOY,

SPEAK TO YOUR SORROW,

AS → THEY TWIST AND TURN IN YOUR DREAMS.

POEM

LIKE BUDDING BRANCHES,

LIKE BEST FRIENDS
(IN A MAZE)

FINDING THEIR WAY

TO THAT **ONE TRUE WORD**
(OR TWO)

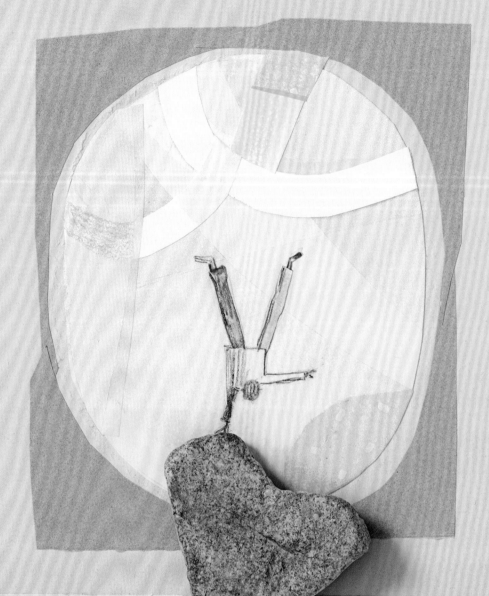

AT THE TIP OF   YOUR HEART

love by the
s at opposite
; the rose was

WHERE
THE
LIGHT
SHINES
THROUGH.

TUNE

WHERE THE WORDS HAVE BEEN WAITING TO SLIDE DOWN YOUR PENCIL

INTO YOUR SMALL PRECIOUS HAND
AND BECOME A VOICE WITH SPUNK.

A Note from Kwame Alexander

To the question *What is poetry?*, a third grader responded, *Poetry is an egg with a horse inside it*. I couldn't have said it better myself. A poem is a small but mighty thing. It has the power to reach inside, to teach us, to ignite our imaginations. Now, more than ever, children need a surefire way to channel their emotions, build their confidence, and discover the world and their place in it. Poetry, in its simplicity, with its accessibility and rhythm, can do all these things instantaneously. Still, it has become the neglected genre. You see, we're kind of afraid of poetry. For so long, we've been taught that poetry is staid, complicated, and unfamiliar, and now many of us believe it. How did this happen, teachers and parents? When did poetry become something intimidating and inaccessible? We have forgotten its power, forgotten that many of the essential joys of poetry are the first ones we experienced as kids discovering the rhythm of language. Forgotten that young children delight in the sounds they make and hear, that the first words that children speak emerge like a repetitive chant. In that way, a child's first words are like a first poem. Deanna Nikaido and I wrote this poem to remind us all that words are fun, that when they are strung together in a particularly beautiful way, we love them. We wrote this book to help us each find our way back to an appreciation of words . . . to remembering the wonder of poetry. . . . We wrote *How to Write a Poem* . . . to show you how to use your words, how to lift your voices . . . how to change the world . . . one stanza at a time.

A Note from Melissa Sweet

One of the best moments in making a book is reading the manuscript for the very first time. I let my imagination run wild, like sowing seeds, knowing anything can happen. Right away this story made me think of circles: big rounded marks, delicate lines, and cut-paper shapes in orbit filling the space. I especially love how Kwame Alexander and Deanna Nikaido began the story with a question and ended with *Now, show us what you've found*. The book comes full circle.

Not long after I began the art, I came across Nikki Giovanni's quote, which you can find at the beginning of the book. She uses the metaphor that "we are all either wheels or connectors . . . which is a bicycle." It was the perfect quote to accompany my circles and spheres looping together.

Usually I make dozens of sketches before starting the final art, but in this case I let the images unfold and surprise me as I went along. It's a thrill to share with you what I found!

This collage art was made with vintage and handmade papers, paint, pencils, printed letterforms, and beach pebbles.